AF433904

curvy girl for the mountain man

emma bray

Copyright © 2024 by Emma Bray

All rights reserved.

No part of this book may be reproduced in any form or by any electronic or mechanical means, including information storage and retrieval systems, without written permission from the author, except for the use of brief quotations in a book review.

one

. . .

Olivia

THE SUN BLAZES down on me as I make my way up the mountain trail, beads of sweat forming on my brow. My legs ache from the strain, but I push forward, determined not to let my curvy body hold me back.

It was my best friend's idea for me to take this solo hiking trip, insisting it would help me escape the stress of my city job. And she was right—for the most part. The further I get from civilization, the more alive I feel.

Painstakingly, *achingly* alive as every muscle in my body screams.

But hey, it's alive, right?

"Who knew nature could be so...invigorating?" I mutter to myself, panting slightly as I maneuver over a large rock.

My thoughts drift to the long hours spent hunched over my desk, the constant demands of my boss, and the endless noise of the city. Out here, all of that fades away, replaced by the sounds of birdsong, rustling leaves, and my own labored breathing.

But, unfortunately, I'm a city girl, and I suck with directions. As the hours pass, I realize I've ventured too far. The path becomes unfamiliar, and a creeping sense of dread begins to overwhelm me.

"Damn it," I curse under my breath, trying to retrace my steps. "I knew I should've stuck to the marked trails."

The anxiety builds inside me, knotting my stomach and quickening my pulse.

I can't shake the feeling that I'm being watched, an unseen presence lurking just out of sight.

"Hello?" I call out hesitantly, knowing full well no one is around to hear me. "Is anyone there?"

As if in response, the ground beneath my feet gives way. I let out a scream as I tumble down the hillside. Pain slices through me as my body is battered by rocks and branches.

My world spins and blurs, the pain intensifying with each jarring impact.

"Help," I whisper, choking on fear and desperation. I don't who the fuck I think I'm talking to. There's no one out here in this god-forsaken place.

And then everything goes black.

Jack

I go still as I hear the rustling.

Something is there.

I know these mountains like the back of my hand, and I also know how important it is to check out any suspicious activity. If you don't, you might just end up with a bear at your doorstep.

So, I make my way through the dense foliage to the source of the noise, and I am *not* prepared for what I find.

A scene that both shocks and intrigues me.

A curvy, beautiful woman lies unconscious at the bottom of a hill, her body bruised and battered.

"Sweet Jesus," I whisper, as I rush over to see about her.

My gaze lingers on her ample breasts, straining against her tight shirt, and my hands itch to reach out and touch them.

I shake my head, disgusted with myself. Fuck, I really have been out here all alone for too many years, haven't I? I need to be making sure she's alive—not ogling her beautiful body while she lays here unconscious.

"Hey, can you hear me?" I ask, gently shaking her shoulder.

No response.

A quick look around, and it's obvious she's alone. But why the fuck was this beautiful creature out here all alone?

I check for a pulse, and then I run my hands all along her body, just to check and make sure nothing is bleeding or broken.

Miraculously, she only seems to have a few surface cuts on her. There's a bit of blood on the back of her head but nothing that should require stitching.

Her pulse is steady, so I scoop her up into my arms without hesitation.

And I know it's crazy as hell, but something settles over me. She feels like a prize, like she's *mine* for the taking.

"Time to get you somewhere safe," I say, startling myself with how low and possessive my voice sounds.

I carry her through the forest, her body pressed against mine, the heat of her a comforting weight against my chest.

She curls into me, nuzzling closer, and my heart starts beating overdrive.

And Christ Almighty, she makes these soft, needy sounds that go straight to my dick.

"Easy now," I murmur, trying to soothe her as I ignore how uncomfortable it suddenly is to walk with this baseball bat in between my legs.

I carry her easily, my cabin not far but secluded enough that no one else would find her if I hadn't. The weight of her in my arms feels right, like she's meant to be there.

As I lay her down on my couch, I can't help but admire the flush on her cheeks and the way her chest heaves as she breathes.

It's not right to want someone this much, especially someone so vulnerable, someone I don't even know. But fuck, I *want* her.

I start a fire in the hearth, the flickering flames casting dancing shadows across the walls, mirroring the turmoil inside me.

She's still unconscious, her lips parted slightly, and I can't tear my eyes away from her.

I should be thinking about first aid, about getting help, but all I can think about is how soft her skin looks, how it would feel under my fingertips.

Jesus, get a grip, man.

I move away to fetch some water and a cloth. I need to clean her wounds. She's got scratches and dirt all over her.

As I dab gently at her face, her eyelids flutter but don't open. My hands shake a little—she's fucking beautiful.

And young. Like a ripe, unpicked cherry.

My cock leaks a stream of precum.

My nostrils flare as I blow out a breath and run a hand along my graying beard.

I'm way too old for a pretty little thing like her. I'm old enough to be her father, for fuck's sake.

I try to push all my salacious thoughts aside and focus on the task at hand.

"Come on, sweetheart, open those eyes for me," I murmur more to myself than to her.

Finally, her eyes flutter open, confusion evident as she gazes around. Her gaze lands on me, and *fuuuck.*

I'm a goner.

two

· · ·

Olivia

DARKNESS. A throbbing ache in my head. I force my heavy eyelids open and blink against harsh sunlight streaming through curtains. Where am I?

I try to sit up, but a wave of dizziness sends me slumping back against the pillows. A rough blanket scratches my skin.

I take a gulping breath and scan the unfamiliar room—plain wood walls, a fireplace with glowing embers, a small kitchen.

Panic rises in my chest. I don't recognize anything.

Worse, I realize with growing horror, I don't

know who I am or how I got here. My mind is terrifyingly blank.

I lick my dry lips and croak out the only thing I remember. "Olivia..."

My name, I think.

Heavy footsteps approach and the door swings open. A large man fills the frame, his rugged face wary beneath a short beard. Piercing blue eyes pin me in place.

"You're awake," he grunts. "About time."

I shrink back. "Who are you? Where am I?" My voice shakes.

He steps closer, looking me over. "Name's Jack. You're at my cabin. I found you passed out in the woods last night."

Woods? Cabin? Nothing sounds familiar. I clutch the blanket tighter. "I don't remember...anything. Except my name. At least, I think it's my name? Olivia."

Jack frowns. "You hit your head pretty hard seems like. Memory loss, I reckon."

Tears sting my eyes. "Do I know you?"

He sighs heavily, rubbing a hand over his stubbled jaw. "Suppose you'll have to stay here til you recover. Nearest town is miles away. I'll look after you best I can."

I'll take that as a no.

"You'll take care of me?" I search his stoic face. "Why?"

"Ain't the type to leave someone helpless. It's the right thing to do." He shrugs like it's simple.

"Thank you," I whisper, both grateful and unnerved to be dependent on this stranger. But then I suppose everyone is a stranger to me now.

Jack just nods. "Rest. I'll get you something to eat." He turns to the kitchen.

I burrow under the covers, my mind reeling. No memories, no idea who I am or my life before this moment. Only the reluctant charity of a gruff mountain man.

An admittedly very hot, super buffed-up, ruggedly sexy mountain man.

Who I don't know, I remind myself.

Fear and confusion swirl inside me. But with no other options, I have no choice but to trust this Jack and pray my memories return soon.

For now, this lonely cabin is my only refuge.

———

Jack

I watch her, those big doe eyes wide with confusion and fear, buried under my old blanket.

Olivia.

That's all she's got, one damn name. She looks fragile, broken like a bird with clipped wings, but there's something about her—a flicker of fire behind that vulnerability. Makes me want to stand guard over it, keep it alive.

I turn away, busying myself with the task of cooking, though the clank of the pots is louder than necessary. I can't let her see the effect she has on me. It's not right to feel this draw towards a woman in her state.

She's lost and alone, and under my roof. The responsibility weighs heavy but there's a part of me that can't deny the thrill of being the one she has to rely on. The one to feed her, clothe her, protect her —it stirs something primal in me.

As the eggs sizzle in the pan, I steal glances at her. Olivia, curled up in a ball, like she's trying to shield herself from the world.

I know that feeling, the need to protect yourself from things you can't even remember.

The cabin is quiet, too quiet. The kind of silence that makes every sound a torment, every thought too loud. I push two plates onto the table and call over my shoulder, "Food's ready."

I watch her as she forces herself out of bed and pads softly towards the table, each step hesitant but determined. Despite her obvious weakness, there's an elegance about her movements that catches me off guard. It stirs something inside me that I haven't felt in years.

"Sit," I instruct gruffly, pulling out a chair for her. She obeys without a word, her gaze low.

"Do you remember anything yet?" I ask as I hand her a fork.

She shakes her head slowly, picking at the scrambled eggs with a slight frown. "Nothing more than before. Just...emptiness."

"Give it time," I say, though the words feel hollow even to me. How do you comfort someone who's lost in their own mind?

The meal passes in relative silence, save for the occasional clink of utensils on plates. There's an undeniable tension—a mix of fear, curiosity, and something darker—thickening the air between us.

Olivia's vulnerability makes me want to reach across the table and pull her into my arms, reassure her that everything will be alright. But I can't—not when she doesn't remember who she is or what brought her here. Not when touching her could be crossing a line I've drawn around us—an unspoken boundary borne out of necessity and propriety.

After we finish eating, I clear the plates, trying to maintain a safe distance. Yet, even as I move away, I feel her eyes on me, studying me. The weight of her gaze is palpable, heavy with things unspoken and feelings yet unearthed.

"Thank you," she says softly, her voice laced with a sadness that tugs at my resolve.

I nod, avoiding her eyes. "You need rest. We can try to jog your memory tomorrow."

"I'm scared," she confesses as she stands, her body swaying slightly. "Scared of not knowing who I am, scared of being here..."

I close the distance between us in two strides, my hands firm on her shoulders. "You're safe here, Olivia. I won't let anything happen to you."

Her breath hitches, and those wide eyes lift to meet mine—a storm of emotions swirling within them. For a moment, we're caught in a silence that speaks louder than words could ever hope to. It's filled with the electric buzz of raw need and restrained desire.

Then, impulsively, dangerously, I pull her closer. Her body fits against mine like she's meant to be there. The feel of her, so close and real, floods my senses—her scent fills my nostrils, her warmth seeps into my skin.

"Jack?" Her voice is a whisper against my chest.

I tighten my grip slightly, wanting nothing more than to lose myself in this moment where only we exist. My voice is rough with barely-contained emotion as I answer, "Yeah?"

The air crackles with tension, our breath mingling in the small gap between us.

Olivia tilts her head back, her eyes searching mine, her lips parted slightly. Every instinct tells me to kiss her, to claim those lips and erase the confusion from her mind with the certainty of my touch.

But I hold back, caught between my need and the ethics of the situation.

Her hand comes up slowly, tentatively, to rest against my chest. The contact is like fire to dry wood, igniting something fierce within me.

She whispers again, a tremor in her voice that matches the one running through her fingers. "I don't know who I am, Jack. But I feel...I feel safe with you."

The words unravel me. It's a trust she shouldn't give so easily—especially not to a man she doesn't remember—but it shackles me to her all the same.

"You are safe," I affirm, my voice low and steady despite the storm raging inside me. "As long as you're here, nothing bad will touch you."

We stand there, locked in an embrace that's both

a comfort and a torment. Her vulnerability wraps around both of us like a thick blanket, heavy with implications that are as dangerous as they are inevitable.

Finally, I gently set her back from me, putting space between us once more. The loss of her warmth leaves me cold, hollowed out. "You should get some sleep," I say, my voice gruff with restraint.

Olivia nods slowly and moves away with a fragile grace that makes my hands itch to reach for her again. I watch her ascend the stairs, each step she takes feels like a small torture, pulling at something deep inside me that yearns to follow, to protect—to possess.

Once she disappears from sight, the stillness of the cabin wraps around me like a straitjacket. I run a hand through my hand and glare down at my aching dick. I feel the sticky precum coating the inside of my jeans. I remember how soft and curvy her sexy body is, and I feel myself grow harder.

Fuck it.

I reach down and unzip my pants.

My hand wraps around my aching dick, the relief immediate but nowhere near enough to quell the raging desire she stirs within me.

I stroke slowly, images of Olivia seared into every movement, every breath that catches slightly in my throat. Her eyes, wide and innocent, yet filled with a raw need that mirrors my own.

I imagine those full tits of hers. Fuck, would she arch her back if I suckled them for her?

And that ripe, juicy pussy…bet she tastes like peaches and cream.

Those luscious globes of her ass…

Those hips that make a man want to plant himself deep inside her and knock her up like a man's supposed to do.

Fuuuck…that does it!

My release comes hard and fast, a guilt-laden pleasure that does nothing to ease the deeper hunger she's kindled within me.

I'm panting, back against the cold kitchen counter, feeling like the lowest sort of man. A protector?

Fuck, *I'm* what she needs protecting from.

three

. . .

Olivia

I SLEEP MOST of the day, dozing in and out, and when I fully wake up again, it's apparently dinner time.

Jack helps me to the little wood table in his kitchen and places a bowl of simple but heart stew in front of me.

We eat mostly in silence, the clinking of our spoons against the bowls punctuating the quiet. I can feel Jack's intense gaze on me, heavy and unyielding, like a physical touch that makes my skin tingle with anticipation.

But I don't know what to say, so I say nothing.

After our meal, I insist on helping Jack clean up, not wanting to feel completely useless. He grudgingly hands me a dishtowel.

As I dry the plates, our hands accidentally brush as he passes me another. Startled, I nearly drop the plate, my cheeks flushing at the brief contact. Jack's hand darts out to steady mine.

"Careful there." His low voice rumbles through me. I glance up to find his striking blue eyes intently focused on me.

"I've got it," I mumble, flustered by his proximity. The air between us feels charged, his rugged masculinity overwhelming in the cozy kitchen.

Averting my gaze, I set the plate down and reach for the next, hyperaware of his solid presence beside me, his body heat radiating. We continue working in charged silence, a palpable tension building.

As I put away the last cup, I turn and nearly collide with Jack's broad chest. "Oh! Sorry, I didn't realize you were right-"

The words die in my throat as his hands grasp my arms to steady me. I suck in a sharp breath.

He's so close I can see the silvery flecks in his blue irises, feel the whisper of his breath on my cheek.

Time seems to still, the air growing heavy. My

pulse pounds as his eyes drop to my parted lips. An anticipatory shiver runs through me.

Is he going to kiss me? Do I *want* him to?

But the charged moment shatters as Jack clears his throat and steps back. "You should get some rest."

He turns away before I can protest. All I've done all day is rest.

I release a shaky exhale, my body humming and confused.

I flee to the bedroom, thrown by the pull I feel towards this mysterious, guarded man.

As I burrow under the covers, I can still feel the imprint of his strong hands, the magnetic attraction between us. My mind races with unanswered questions, but one thing is alarmingly clear—my rescuer affects me in ways I don't understand.

And I crave more.

"Watch your footing on these rocks." Jack's deep voice carries over the rushing of the nearby stream as he guides me across the slippery stepping stones. His large, calloused hand engulfs mine, warm and strong. I grip it tightly, my heart pounding as I focus on not losing my balance.

I woke up this morning to Jack announcing that it would be good for me to get out of the house, and I couldn't agree more.

Safely across, he releases my hand and I immediately miss his touch.

Get a grip, Olivia. So what if he's the most ruggedly handsome man you've ever laid eyes on. You barely know him.

"I'll show you how to collect kindling for the fire." Jack sets down the fishing gear and crouches to gather an armful of small dry twigs and branches scattered on the forest floor. I watch the muscles ripple beneath his flannel shirt, imagining what his bare skin would feel like under my fingertips...

I shake my head, dispelling the dangerous thought. "Like this?" I ask, bending to pick up some sticks.

"Yep, just make sure they're dry. Damp wood won't catch."

As we work side by side, the silence stretches between us, but it's not uncomfortable. There's an easiness to being in his presence, even though I hardly know anything about him.

"Jack?" I venture after a while. "Can I ask you something personal?"

He pauses, his blue eyes searching mine before he nods once. "Go ahead."

I wet my lips, wondering if I'm overstepping. "What made you decide to live out here all alone? In the mountains, away from everything?"

Jack is quiet for a long moment. Then he sighs heavily, his gaze distant. "I needed to get away after my parents died," he says gruffly. "The memories, the pitying looks, all the reminders...it was too much. Out here, things are simpler. Quieter."

My throat tightens with sympathy. "I'm so sorry. I shouldn't have pried."

"It's alright. It was a long time ago." But I can see the old grief still lingers in the taut lines of his face.

Impulsively, I reach out to squeeze his arm. He glances down at my hand in surprise.

Electricity zings through me at the contact and I quickly let go, my cheeks heating.

"We should head back," Jack says, clearing his throat. "Storm clouds are rolling in."

As we trek through the dense trees back toward the cabin, I find myself intensely aware of his solid presence at my back, and I know with startling clarity that something has shifted between us.

Something that both terrifies and thrills me.

Back at the cabin, the tension between us is palpable, the very air charged with unspoken desire. Jack builds a fire in the hearth as I prepare our simple dinner, hyper-conscious of every accidental brush of hands, every heated glance.

We eat in charged silence, the crackling of the flames and patter of rain against the roof the only sounds. I feel his gaze on me like a physical caress, and it takes all my willpower not to squirm in my seat.

After dinner, the space between us feels smaller, almost suffocating with intensity. Jack clears the dishes without a word, his movements deliberate, controlled. I watch him, fascinated by the play of muscles under his shirt as he bends to stoke the fire. The way he commands the small cabin space, it makes me wonder if he approaches *everything* in life with the same meticulousness.

I hear a clap of thunder outside, a mirror to the storm brewing within me. My heartbeat is a frantic drum in my ears as he approaches, the heat from his body mingling with the warmth from the fire.

He stands close, too close, and my breath catches in my throat as his eyes search mine, dark and intense. "Olivia," he murmurs, his voice low and rough. There's a question in his gaze, a silent plea for something I'm not sure I can name.

I swallow hard, the air thick with the scent of rain and woodsmoke. "Jack," I whisper back, unable to form any more words. My voice trembles as much as my hands, the hunger in his eyes stripping away any thought of resistance.

He steps even closer, our bodies almost touching, his breath warm against my face. "I want you," he confesses, each word laced with a raw need that reverberates through my bones. "I've wanted you since the moment you stumbled into my life, looking lost and so damn breakable."

His admission hangs heavy between us, charged like the storm outside. His fingers brush lightly against my jaw, tracing the line of my skin gently, achingly. I tilt my head back, surrendering to the touch, to the electric shock his skin against mine sends coursing through me. His other hand finds the small of my back, pulling me closer until there's no air between us, only the mingling of our breaths and the shared heat of our bodies.

"I shouldn't want this...but I do," he continues, his voice a husky whisper that stirs the flames inside me even further. His eyes are an abyss, pulling me in deeper with every passing second, and I'm powerless to resist the pull.

His lips hover over mine, tantalizingly close, and the anticipation twists a hot knot in my stomach.

And then lightning cracks, loud and harsh.

I jump, and the spell is broken.

Jack clears his throat and hangs his head. He mumbles something about needing to check his shed out back.

And before I can protest, he's gone.

Again.

four

. . .

Jack

I LEAD Olivia up the rocky trail, my hand grasping hers tightly. The dark clouds gathering overhead make me quicken our pace.

Maybe this impromptu hike wasn't the best idea, but I had to do something. Had to get out of that cabin before I did something stupid.

Like bending her juicy ass over the kitchen table and fucking her to kingdom come.

"Jack, it looks like a storm is coming..." Olivia's voice quavers slightly.

I flash her a reassuring grin. "We'll be fine,

sweetheart. I know these trails like the back of my hand. Trust me."

But the skies open up minutes later, pelting us with heavy raindrops. Olivia yelps, pressing herself against me. I wrap an arm around her curvy waist, pulling her close.

"There's a small cave up ahead where we can take shelter," I tell her. "Come on!"

We dash through the downpour, finding refuge in a shallow rocky alcove. Both of us are soaked to the bone, shivering. Olivia's thin t-shirt clings to her curves, revealing the lacy bra underneath. I swallow hard.

"Looks like we might be stuck here a while," I murmur, peeling off my dripping jacket.

Olivia trembles, teeth chattering, arms crossed over her chest. "I'm f-freezing."

"Come here." I open my arms to her. "We need to share body heat."

She only hesitates a moment before nestling against me. I rub her back and arms briskly, trying to infuse some warmth into her slight frame.

Her soft scent fills my nose—vanilla and something uniquely Olivia.

It's intoxicating.

Arousing.

And I try to make myself think of anything else even as I feel my dick growing in my pants.

Fucking hell, I'm perpetually hard around this girl.

But could any man blame me with all these curves pressed up against me?

How about them Jets?

Isn't that what guys do when they're trying to get their out-of-control boners back in the cage?

How about them Jets?

No surprise, the shit ain't working.

We sit huddled together, watching the storm rage outside our little haven.

Olivia eventually stops shaking. Her breathing slows. I feel the soft swell of her breasts pressing against my chest with each inhale.

My cock grows even harder—if that's even possible. Desire unfurls deep in my core.

Christ, I *want* her.

I've wanted her from the first moment I saw her. But she's been through so much already...

"Thank you for taking care of me, Jack," Olivia whispers, tilting her face up to mine. In the dim light, her eyes glimmer with trust and vulner-ability.

"I'll always take care of you, Olivia," I vow as I

cup her delicate jaw in my palm. "You never have to be afraid when you're with me."

She stares at me.

I stare at her.

And then I'm leaning down. Fuck, I can't stop this. I feel her breath hot against my lips, and then…

I press my lips against her.

Fucking *heaven*.

Her lips are satin soft, parting on a sigh. I pull her tighter against me, angling my head to deepen the kiss. She meets me with equal hunger, her tongue sliding along mine, unpracticed, innocent. Just the thought that she might be a virgin sends parks of pleasure shooting through my veins.

The intensity builds swiftly between us, greedy hands roaming, pulses racing.

I want to devour her.

Possess every inch of her sweet, curvy body.

But I gently wrench my mouth away, both of us left panting. We can't rush this. When I take her, it will be in a bed, with sheets twisted from our passion, not in the rough dirt of a makeshift campsite. This isn't the place for her first time. She deserves better than that.

I groan internally, fighting every primal urge in my body.

Her eyes are wide, lips swollen from our kiss, looking every bit the innocent doe in the headlights, yet there's a flush of arousal on her cheeks that tells me she wants this too. "Jack," she breathes out, her voice a mix of desire and apprehension.

"Olivia," I murmur back, my voice rough with restraint. My hands frame her face, thumbs caressing her cheeks.

And that's when I hear it.

A low growl, much like that of an angry cat.

I look to the mouth of the cave, and every tendon in my body snaps to attention.

A bobcat.

The beast's eyes, golden and gleaming with a predatory hunger, fix on Olivia.

My heart slams against my chest like it wants out, like it knows the danger this creature poses to her.

Instantly, I'm in front of her, one arm shielding her body from the looming threat.

"Stay behind me," I command, my voice a low growl to match the bobcat's menacing stance.

Olivia nods, her body trembling against mine, her breaths coming in sharp, scared huffs. I can feel her gripping the fabric of my shirt, her fingers digging in with fear.

"Don't worry, I've got you," I whisper back to her, trying to infuse calm into the charged air.

The bobcat edges closer, its eyes never leaving Olivia. The rain outside has muted, casting an eerie silence over us—except for the pounding of my heart and Olivia's shallow breathing.

I stand tall, making myself as large as possible, staring down the bobcat. I hiss at it, my body calm despite the adrenaline surging through my veins.

The bobcat snarls in response, but I hold my ground, locking eyes with it.

If there's one thing I've learned out here, it's how to handle the wildlife without harming it. Wild animals aren't evil. They're just doing what they're meant to do, protecting their territory and themselves.

Minutes stretch like hours under the weight of the standoff. Finally, with one last disdainful glance, the bobcat turns and disappears into the shadows of the forest.

I let out a breath I didn't realize I was holding and turn back to Olivia. Her face is pale but flushed from our close encounter and our earlier embrace.

"Is it gone?" she asks, her voice quivering.

"Yeah, it's gone," I confirm, pulling her into a tight hug. "You're safe now."

Her arms wrap around me tightly, and she

buries her face in my chest. "Thank you," she mumbles against my soaked shirt.

"We should get home, though," I suggest gently as I notice that the storm has passed. The rain has abated to just a few sprinkles here and there. "Just to be safe."

Olivia nods against me, still clinging to my shirt for a sense of security.

As we walk back down the trail, her hand finds mine, her fingers intertwining with mine tightly.

"I was so scared," she admits softly as we navigate our way through the thick underbrush, still slick with rain. The moon, breaking through the clouds, casts a silver glow over us, giving the woods an ethereal feel.

"I know," I reply, squeezing her hand reassuringly. "But I meant what I said—I've got you."

She looks up at me through long

lashes, her eyes glistening with a mixture of fear and something deeper, more intense. "I believe you," she says, her voice barely above a whisper. "I really do."

The rest of the walk is silent except for the sound of our footsteps and the occasional distant call of a night bird. The intimacy of the moment wraps around us like the fog that starts to settle between the trees.

Every glance she gives me, every slight squeeze of her hand sends a current racing through my blood, stoking the fire that started with a simple kiss and has been fueled by danger and desire.

As we reach the edge of the woods, the sight of the cabin emerging through the fog sends a thrill of relief through me.

Yet, there's a part of me that doesn't want this night to end, this forced closeness to break. The danger has passed, but the desire hangs between us, palpable and demanding attention.

We step onto the porch, and I unlock the door, pushing it open. The inside of the cabin is cozy and warm, a stark contrast to the frigid atmosphere of the forest.

I flick on the lights, flooding the room with a warm glow, and turn to see Olivia shivering slightly from the dampness of her clothes.

"Here, let me get you something warm to change into," I say, guiding her toward the fireplace where the embers are still alive with heat. "You'll catch your death in those wet things."

Olivia nods, her teeth chattering a bit as she peels off the soaked layers. She stands there, vulnerable and exquisite, her skin glistening under the amber light of the fire, every curve and contour highlighted in the flickering shadows. My breath catches in my throat, the primal part of me roaring to life as I watch her.

I can't move. I'm rooted to the spot. My cock surges to full life again, and I ball my hands into fists, trying desperately to restrain myself.

But it's a fight I'm never going to win.

five

· · ·

Olivia

"OLIVIA." My name is a deep rumble in Jack's chest.

Slowly, I raise my eyes to his. The intensity I find there steals my breath.

His eyes rove over my naked form with raw, primal *hunger*.

I don't know what possessed me to just strip down in front of him right here, but I did, and the way his voice is all hoarse and his wild sends a thrill through me.

In the firelight, his rugged features are cast in

flickering shadows, making him look almost dangerous.

Untamed.

But what else could I expect from a man who could stare down a bobcat?

My pulse pounds as he takes a step toward me, then another. I'm caught, ensnared by his unwavering stare. He reaches out, callused fingers grazing my cheek with surprising gentleness.

"If you want me to stop, say so now," he warns, his voice low and rough with restraint. "Because in another minute, I won't be able to."

I should put a halt to this. It's reckless, impulsive. I barely know this man. But I'm tired of being cautious, of denying myself. For once, I want to give in to my desires, consequences be damned.

And I don't know how I know that I always play it safe when I can't remember anything about myself—just that it's a feeling.

"Don't stop," I whisper, tilting my face into his touch. "Please."

Something fierce and hungry ignites in his eyes. "Olivia," he growls and captures my mouth with his.

Jack's kiss is demanding, consuming, his lips moving against mine with urgent need. I cling to his broad shoulders, dizzy with the onslaught of sensation.

His tongue delves into my mouth, tasting, *claiming*. I've never been kissed like this before, with such raw, desperate hunger.

At least I don't *think* I have. I would know something like that, wouldn't I?

It's thrilling and terrifying all at once.

A low moan escapes me as his hands skim down my sides to settle on my hips, pulling me flush against the hard plane of his body.

Every nerve ending sparks to life, hyperaware of each point of contact between us. I thread my fingers through his salt-and-pepper hair, deepening the kiss, matching his fervor with my own rising passion.

He tears his mouth from mine to trail searing kisses along my jaw, my neck. "You have no idea what you do to me," he rasps against my skin. "From the moment I saw you..."

His teeth graze my earlobe and I gasp, arching into him. "I couldn't stop thinking about you. Wanting you." His hands slip over the underside of my breasts, calloused palms igniting flames in their wake.

"Jack..." His name falls from my lips like a plea.

I'm drowning in sensation, lost to anything but his touch, his scent, the heat of his body against mine.

"Tell me you want this," he demands, his breath hot on my neck. "That you want *me*." His hips press into mine, letting me feel the evidence of his desire, hard and insistent.

When I don't immediately answer, he shakes his head, and a torrent of words pour from him, "Fuck, I should stop this. I'm old enough to be your daddy, girl. Do you understand that? You're so young and pretty and motherfucking delectable." He squeezes my waist as if to punctuate his words.

And I don't know where it comes from, but I say before I can even think about it, "Then be my daddy."

He makes a strangled sound, and something fierce and possessive flares in his eyes. "You're *mine*," he growls before he claims my mouth again in a bruising kiss.

———

Jack

Her words ignite something primal in me.

Then be my daddy.

Fuck, it's like a match to tinder within my veins. I never knew I had a daddy kink. Still don't know that that's what you'd call it. I just have an Olivia kink. Anything my curvy little beauty wants, that's what she'll get. And if she wants a daddy, then hot damn sign me up.

I'm consumed by her—every soft curve, each whispered word fuels the fire that rages uncontrollably inside me.

I don't hesitate any longer.

I can't.

My hands explore her body with newfound ownership, each touch asserting my claim. Her skin is soft under my rough fingers, delicate yet burning with the same ferocious need that's overtaking me.

"Mine," I affirm again, as if speaking it into existence will somehow secure her to me irrevocably. I trail kisses down her throat, each one a seal of possession, and she tilts her head back, giving me freer access, surrending to me.

Mine.

Her hands claw at my back, pulling me closer until there's no space left between us. I quickly free my cock from my pants and rub it up and down against her pussy.

"Fuck, that thing is juicy. Just like I knew it would be," I hiss.

The friction of our bodies moving together sends shockwaves through my core. I'm teetering on the edge of control, every cell in my body screaming for release.

But I hold back, because this isn't just about finding release—it's about marking every inch of her as mine.

With deliberate intent, I push her gently against the wall. The cool surface contrasts sharply with the heat of our bodies as I lift her thigh to wrap around my hip. Her breath catches. Those wide eyes lock onto mine, reflecting a storm of emotions that I feel mirrored in my chest.

"I need you," I confess, the words raw and laden with a truth that terrains beyond mere physical need. It's deeper—elementary and all-consuming.

"Jack... please," she breathes out, her voice laced with urgency and something like desperation. That plea shatters the last vestige of restraint within me.

I capture her lips once more, sealing the promise made in our shared breaths and whispers. I pick her up, and her legs wrap around me instinctively as I carry her over the bed.

I'm a man of my word, and I vowed to myself

that I would take her on a bed like she deserves, worship her like the curvy fucking goddess she is.

She whimpers when I lay her on the bed and pull back from her, but I shush with a kiss against her soft stomach.

And then I fall to my knees and kiss my way down to the center of her thighs, to that holy altar I want to worship at.

"Jack, Jack," her voice is breathless, a mix of need and surrender that fires me up further.

I look up from my position between her thighs, her eyes glazed with fervor meet mine, and it's like a fucking punch to the gut—this girl owns me as much as I own her.

I can't help but smile against the softness of her inner thigh before I turn my attention back to the prize. My tongue slides over her pussy, tasting her, savoring the sweetness that is uniquely Olivia.

And then I flick my tongue over her swollen clit.

She moans louder, fingers threading through my hair, pushing me closer as if she can't get enough.

"More, Jack, I need more," she gasps out, her voice cracking with the intensity of her desire. Her hips buck against my face, seeking further contact, urging me to deepen the exploration.

I oblige without hesitation because denying her anything feels like denying myself oxygen.

I dive deeper, my tongue writing promises inside her that both of us know I intend to keep.

Her taste is addictive—a pure aphrodisiac—and her sounds, those delicious moans and cries, are the sweetest symphony to my ears. They drive me wild, fueling my arousal to near unbearable levels. I'm humping the air because God help me if I can keep still.

"Please, Daddy..." she whispers in a throaty beg that snaps the restraint I've been clinging to. Her calling me that, with such needy innocence, rips through any remaining hesitation and ignites a feral hunger within.

I rise up, aligning myself with her trembling body, and with one smooth thrust, I bury myself deep inside her.

I feel her hymen rip, and I let out an animalistic roar of satisfaction at know I'm the first and only man who will ever have her this way.

She cries out—a sound so raw and pure—her back arching off the bed as if reaching for salvation.

I anchor her down with my body, making sure she feels every inch of me, every beat of my heart.

"Mine," I growl into her ear, punctuating each

word with a deep thrust that has her whispering affirmations and unraveling under the wave of pleasure that crahes over us simultaneously. My cock is leaking precum like a sieve, and it's taking everything in me to keep my spilling my load in her prematurely.

"Yours, Jack, always yours," she gasps between breaths, her nails digging into my back, marking me as much as I mark her.

The room is thick with the scent of sex and sweat, and the only sounds are our ragged breaths and the slap of skin against skin.

I move with a relentless urgency, driven by an instinctual need to claim her, to fuse our bodies and souls into one unbreakable entity.

The intensity of it pushes me closer and closer to the edge, every thrust deeper and harder than the last.

Her legs tighten around my waist, pulling me even closer, if that's even possible. Our connection deepens beyond the physical joining—spiraling into something neither of us could have anticipated.

I go deeper than before and capture her gasp with my mouth, kissing her deeply, fucking into her mouth like I am her body.

Each thrust is met with a welcoming pull from

her, inviting me deeper—not just into her body but into the very essence of who she is.

The world falls away. There is nothing but Olivia and the intoxicating bind she has tangled me in.

Each moan, each arch from her not only takes us higher but binds us tighter.

Closer to climax, I slow down. She lets out a whimper of protest, but I cup her face and look into her beautiful eyes. "Ssh, baby, I want to make this moment last. I want to remember it forever. The moment you became mine, you beautiful goddess."

"I am yours," she confirms, her beautiful eyes staring back into mine.

"Daddy," she adds with a mischevous little smirk.

Holy fuck! I lose it then.

"Fuck, baby, you know what that does to me, don't you? You know Daddy can't hold back when you're throwing that sweet thing up on him and calling him 'Daddy', don't you? You want it, baby? Cause here it comes, sweetheart. All Daddy's juices just for you, baby doll."

And then with a groan that feels like it's coming straight from my soul, I release my sperm into her. My balls draw up tight, my cock pulses over and over again, violently dumping stream after stream of cum into her waiting pussy.

And when I feel her pussy clenching around mine, signaling her orgasm, that only sets me off again. More cum shoots from my head, filling her up until it's leaking out onto the bed between us.

Still, I remain inside her, unwilling to break this connection that feels more vital than air.

"Mine," I whisper as I plant a protective kiss on her forehead.

This girl is *mine*.

six

· · ·

Olivia

A FACE FLASHES before my eyes. Strong jaw, sandy blonde hair, piercing blue eyes boring into mine.

I gasp, reality flooding back as the mysterious man fades away.

Who was he?

The intensity in his gaze felt so real, so familiar. Like a distant memory clawing to the surface.

I shake my head, trying to clear the confusing images.

Focus, Olivia.

But I can't shake the feeling that he was someone important to me.

Someone I cared for deeply.

Suddenly, Jack's voice cuts through my reverie. "Olivia? You okay?"

"Y-yeah, I'm fine," I stammer, avoiding his concerned gaze. How can I explain that I just had a flashback of another man? Especially after what we just did? "Just tired."

Jack stares at me for a long moment, and I swear he can see right through me.

But he doesn't press the issue. Instead, he just nods as he pulls my head to lay back on his chest.

I nod absently too, my mind still reeling.

Who are you? I silently implore the nameless man in my mind. *And what were you to me?*

———

Jack

I scroll through the search results, my eyes scanning for any scrap of information about Olivia's past.

Then I see it. Something that makes my heart fall.

A photo of Olivia with some other fucking guy.

I take in his quintessential good lucks. His sandy blonde hair. Blue eyes.

I instantly hate him.

Anger surges through my veins, hot and potent. I slam the laptop shut.

I don't need to see any more. Don't want to know who he was to her.

Olivia walks in, her brow furrowed. "Everything alright, Jack?"

"Fine," I grit out. She flinches at my harsh tone, but I can't bring myself to care. Not when images of her with him cloud my vision.

"Well, I was thinking we could-" she starts.

"Not now, Olivia." The words come out harsher than I intend. Her eyes widen, hurt swimming in their depths.

Shit.

"I just...I can't right now." I turn away, hating myself but unable to stop.

She's silent for a long moment.

Then she turns and flees the room, a soft, broken sound escaping her.

I'm instantly remorseful, my heart tearing in two.

I *hurt* her. My girl. I never want to hurt her.

I should go after her.

Explain.

Apologize.

But I can't move, jealousy and fear freezing me in place as she runs from me.

The sound of the door slamming finally jolts me into action.

I can't let her go, not like this.

I race after her, my heart pounding in time with my footsteps. I find her outside, her curvy form wracked with sobs. The sight cleaves me in two.

"Olivia," I rasp, reaching for her.

She whirls to face me, tears streaking her flushed cheeks. "Why, Jack? Why are you pushing me away?"

I swallow hard. "I'm not, baby. I would never. But what are you not telling me?"

She had a memory. I know it. I could tell by the look on her face, and her face betrays her again right now.

Her brow furrows. "What? I don't..."

"Who was he, Olivia?" The question rips from my throat, raw and aching.

She shakes her head helplessly. "I don't know! I can't remember!" A fresh wave of tears overtakes her.

I pull her into my arms, crushing her to my chest. "I'm sorry. God, I'm so sorry. I just...the thought of you with someone else..." I shudder.

She clings to me, her tears soaking my shirt. "You're the only one I want, Jack. The only one I see. I can't remember my past! And I don't even want to! Not if it takes me from you!" She lets out another sob.

A groan rises in my throat. I capture her face in my hands, wiping away her tears with my thumbs. "You're *mine*, Olivia. No matter what. *Mine.*"

Then I claim her mouth in a searing kiss, pouring every ounce of my jealousy, my longing, my desperate *need* into the hot slide of our lips.

She meets me with equal fervor, her fingers tangling in my hair.

I lift her, and she wraps her legs around my waist. Never breaking the kiss, I carry her back inside, kicking the door shut behind us.

The past falls away as we lose ourselves in the heat of the present, in each other.

I worship her body with hands and mouth, learning every curve, every hollow. She arches beneath me, pleading for more, calling me *Daddy*.

I answer with a slow, deep thrust that has us both crying out.

We move together, our bodies finding our rhythm.

My cock pistons in and out of her. Her pussy sucks me in tight with each thrust.

Squeezing.

Milking.

Oh fuck!

I explode, shooting my cum deep inside her.

In the afterglow, I gather her close, pressing fervent kisses to her damp skin. "I love you, Olivia. No matter what happened before, you're *mine* now."

My voice sounds as desperate as I feel, but fuck if I can help it.

I can't live without her now.

She's *mine*.

seven

. . .

Jack

SWEAT DRIPS down my back as I hike through the dense forest, thoughts of Olivia consuming me. Her soft skin, bright eyes, the way she feels in my arms...

I need to focus. Find more firewood before the sun sets and the temperature drops.

A twig snaps behind me. I whirl around, hand reaching for my knife, ready to confront a bear or mountain lion. But it's not an animal.

My heart falls.

It's a group of men, fanned out in a search party formation. My heart clenches.

They're looking for *her*.

My Olivia.

The one in the lead is tall, broad-shouldered, classically handsome.

It's him. The man from the picture.

I ball my hands into fists.

He's exactly the kind of man a woman like Olivia deserves. Not some washed-up recluse like me.

"You there!" the man calls out. "Have you seen a young woman? Brown hair, green eyes?" He holds up a photo.

It's her.

Smiling, radiant.

My fist tightens around the knife handle. I could lie. Lead them in the wrong direction. Keep Olivia to myself a little longer.

But it wouldn't be right.

She doesn't belong to me, no matter how much I wish she did.

"Yeah," I say gruffly. "She's at my cabin. Quarter mile that way." I point to the east, every word feeling like a knife to the gut.

The man's eyes narrow. "Your cabin? What the hell is she doing there?"

I bristle at his accusing tone. "I found her. In the woods. Injured. Been nursing her back to health."

He gives me a once-over, clearly finding me lacking.

I clench my jaw, fighting the urge to lay him out. But Olivia wouldn't want that.

So, I turn and stride back toward the cabin, hearing the search party fall into step behind me.

My heart cracks more with every step with take.

God, can I do this?

As we approach the cabin, Olivia bursts out the door. Her eyes widen, flicking from me to the man behind me.

"Olivia, thank God!" He rushes forward, and she takes a step back, scared, confused.

I take a step forward, ready to intervene.

But then she blinks rapidly, and recognition dawns on her face.

My chest tightens. I feel like I'm going to have a heart attack.

"Nate?" her voice is full of wonder. "Oh my God, Nate!" She throws herself into his arms and clings to him, tears streaming down her face.

I look away, gut twisting. I knew this moment would come. That she'd remember her old life and leave. Deep down, I knew.

And it hurts like a son-of-a-bitch.

Unable to stand there and watch their reunion a second longer, I turn and head into the woods.

The image of her in his arms is seared into my brain.

I find a log and sink down onto it, head in my hands. She's better off. A woman like her doesn't belong in a place like this.

With a man like me.

I hang my head low and do something I haven't done in a long time—since my parents died, in fact.

I cry.

eight

· · ·

Jack

MOONLIGHT FILTERS through the trees as I trudge back to the cabin, shoulders hunched against the chill night air. Twigs snap beneath my boots, echoing the hollow ache in my chest. Hours spent wandering the woods trying to drive Olivia from my mind. The image of her in another man's arms, laughing, smiling in a way she never will with me again.

I shake my head, jaw clenched. It's over before it even began. I never should have let myself hope, never should have believed her lingering gazes and soft sighs meant anything more.

Not when she had a whole life waiting for her. Why would she willingly stay here with me in the middle of nowhere?

My cabin comes into view. I climb the porch steps, fumbling for the doorknob with numb fingers.

The door swings open, and I freeze, my hand still suspended in mid-air.

Olivia sits curled on the couch, haloed by the glow of dying embers in the fireplace. Her eyes meet mine, dark with some emotion I can't read.

"Jack," she says softly. "Where have you been?"

I swallow hard. "Out. What are you doing here, Olivia?"

She stands, wrapping her arms around herself as she takes a tentative step closer. "You left so suddenly earlier. I was worried." Her brow furrows. "Why did you go?"

My pulse thunders in my ears. I should lie, make some excuse. But I'm stunned by her presence, and the truth spills out, raw and painful. "Seeing you with someone else—with him—would drive me crazy," I rasp. "I could't...can't...I watch you in the arms of another man."

Her lips part in surprise and something that looks like dawning realization. She takes another step toward me, close enough now that I can see the amber flecks in her hazel eyes, smell vanilla scent.

"Jack," she breathes. "That man...he's not who you think."

I stare at her, my brows furrowed now.

My heart starts beating in overdrive.

I'm scared to hope. Afraid to believe this isn't another dream that will dissolve like mist come morning.

Her hand comes up to rest over my racing heart.

Her touch sears me, even through the fabric of my shirt. My skin feels too tight, stretched thin over the maelstrom churning inside me.

"That man is my brother, Jack. Not my boyfriend. There's not anyone else...just you."

The words hang suspended between us for a breathless moment. Then something snaps inside me, the last fraying thread of my control. I surge forward, capturing her face between my hands as I claim her mouth in a searing kiss.

She meets me with matching hunger, fingers fisting in my hair to pull me closer.

I groan into the kiss, drunk on the taste of her, the feel of her soft curves molding to my hardness. Those curves I thought I would never feel again.

Tears prick my eyes as I rasp out, "Thought I

lost you…couldn't deal with it…" I trail off, my throat suddenly too tight to speak.

"You'll never lose me, Daddy," she tells me softly, and that's all I need to hear.

I smash my lips to her agains, and then with a growl, I lift her into my arms, not breaking the kiss as I carry her to the plush rug in front of the fireplace.

I lay her down gently, covering her body with mine. She arches up to meet me, hands tugging impatiently at my clothes.

I strip us both with desperate efficiency, needing to feel her skin against mine. When there are no more barriers between us, I pull back just enough to look into her eyes, dark and hazy with desire.

"I love you, Olivia," I tell her fiercely. "I've always loved you. Only you."

"Show me," she whispers. "Fuck me, Daddy."

Primal satisfaction roars through me at her words. I set about doing just that, worshipping every inch of her with hands and mouth until she's writhing beneath me, begging for more.

And when I finally sink into her welcoming heat, joining us as one, it feels like coming home.

We move together, giving and taking pleasure, stoking the flames of our passion higher and higher until the world disappears, narrowing to just this—skin and sweat, sighs and moans, two hearts beating in perfect sync.

I breathe her name like a prayer when I find my release, and she shatters in my arms a moment later with a cry of ecstasy.

In the afterglow, I gather her close, savoring the feel of her in my arms. She snuggles into me with a contented hum, pressing a tender kiss over my heart.

"I love you too, Jack," she murmurs drowsily, lashes fluttering. "Always will."

I tighten my arms around her and let my eyes drift shut, at peace for the first time in my life.

This is where I belong. With her, my Olivia, in this perfect moment stretching into forever.

Nothing else matters. Just us, and this love that will never fade.

epilogue

. . .

One year later

Olivia

I GAZE out the window at the majestic, snow-capped mountains, feeling a fluttering kick inside my round belly. Jack comes up behind me, his strong arms wrapping around my waist, hands resting on my pregnant stomach.

"How are my gorgeous wife and baby doing this morning?" he murmurs, nuzzling my neck. His stubble tickles my sensitive skin, making me shiver with desire.

"We're perfect," I breathe, leaning back into his

solid warmth. "This is everything I never knew I always wanted."

Jack spins me around and claims my mouth in a searing kiss, his tongue plundering and possessing. I moan wantonly, my body instantly alight for him, always for him.

He pulls back, eyes blazing with lust and love. "I will never get enough of you, Olivia. Never."

In one smooth motion, he scoops me up and strides toward our bedroom. He lays me gently on our king-sized bed and slowly peels off my cotton nightgown, reverence in his every touch.

"So beautiful," he rasps, voice husky with need. "I love seeing you ripe with my child. Knowing I put that baby in your belly."

Anticipation skitters down my spine as he spreads my thighs. The first swipe of his tongue through my slick folds has me crying out his name. He licks and sucks at my swollen clit, pushing me higher, winding me tighter.

"That's it, baby. Let go. Come all over Daddy's face," he growls against my throbbing flesh.

My climax explodes through me and I shatter, wave after wave of ecstasy crashing over me. Jack laps up every drop as if I'm his favorite treat.

He surges up my body to capture my lips, letting me taste my pleasure.

"Fuck, you taste so good, sweetheart," he groans into my mouth. "I could feast on this pretty pussy all day long."

His filthy words make me clench with need. "Please Jack...I need you inside me. *Now*."

Desperation edges my voice. The desire to have him stretching me, filling me, consumes my every thought.

He reaches down to fist his enormous cock, running the broad head through my drenched slit.

"Is this what you want, my naughty girl? You want me to stuff this big dick in your tight little cunt?"

"God yes!" I keen, arching my hips to take him deeper. "Fuck me, Daddy! Fuck me hard!"

With a savage growl, he drives forward, impaling me on his thick shaft in one powerful thrust. I scream out at the exquisite pleasure.

He pulls out slowly, dragging his cock along my fluttering walls before slamming back in, fucking me with deep, pounding strokes.

"So fucking tight," Jack snarls, his hips snapping relentlessly as he pounds into my soaked heat. "This greedy little pussy was made for my cock. No one else will ever touch you. You're mine, Olivia. All mine."

"Yes, yes, yes!" I chant mindlessly, lost to the

overwhelming bliss of his possession. "I'm yours, only yours! Please don't stop!"

He hooks my knees over his elbows, spreading me wider, fucking me deeper. I feel every thick, pulsing inch of him stretching me, owning me, branding me as his.

Pleasure builds and builds, coiling tighter and tighter. My cunt clenches down on his relentless cock, milking the rigid length. Pressure builds at the base of my spine as my climax approaches, threatening to consume me.

"That's it, my sweet little wife. Come on my cock," Jack commands gruffly, hammering into me even harder. "Drench me with your cum. I'm going to come too, baby. Better be glad you're already pregnant, or Daddy would for sure knock you up with this big load he's about to give you."

His dirty demands send me flying over the edge. My pussy spasms violently around him as I shatter, screaming his name. Jack pistons his hips a few more times before throwing his head back with a primal roar, flooding my clenching channel with his hot seed.

He collapses on top of me, careful not to crush my swollen stomach, both of us gasping for breath.

I cling to his sweat-slicked shoulders as little aftershocks roll through me.

"You're mine, Olivia. Always. I'll never stop loving you, wanting you," he pants against my neck

Joy expands in my chest, blending with the deep satiation only Jack, my husband, my *daddy*, can provide. "Forever," I vow. "You and me and our family, forever."

Want a free book from Emma Bray? Go to www.authoremmabray.com.

Keep reading for an excerpt from the next Curvy Girl Romance Short, Curvy Girl for the Billionaire.

Chapter 1

Charlie

I slip through the throng of midday pedestrians. The pulse of the city synchronizes with the throb of a headache I'm nursing.

It's another day where every penny clings to

each other for dear life in my bank account. Charlotte "Charlie" Greene is my name, though the second part feels like a cruel joke. Green usually means go, or growth, or cash—things that seem just out of reach at the moment.

I started my event planning business the day I turned eighteen. A generous relative left me a sizable sum of cash, but it wasn't enough to live on for the rest of my life, so I thought I would do the smart thing and invest in a business doing something I loved.

It, coupled with a meticulous business plan, was enough to convince the bank that I meant business and secure the rest of the capital I needed to get my dream underway.

Three years later and my business is growing, but so are my bills. And rent here in the city isn't cheap. I just need a few more really good gigs and then I'll be out of debt and it'll all be profit.

Until then, the struggle is real.

My phone buzzes against the soft flesh of my hip, buried deep within the confines of my purse.

Shit, what now?

Fuck it, I'll check it later.

There are schedules to triple-check, venues to scout, and dreams to chase—even if they're wearing me thin.

The coffee shop on the corner is my first stop. It's not a luxury, but a necessity. The barista, a boy barely out of his teens, knows my order by heart. His eyes linger on the curves that my pencil skirt hugs unapologetically, but it's a look I've learned to ignore. I need caffeine, not a flirtation.

"Large Americano, extra shot," he recites, like a prayer offered to the goddess of overwork.

"Keep the change," I say, leaving a couple of dollars on the counter—my attempt at generosity, even when it hurts. I pivot on a heel, the air around me clinging to my body, heavy with the scent of freshly ground coffee beans and frothed milk.

Back on the street, I pass storefronts with mannequins dressed in clothes too expensive for their stillness, and restaurants where laughter spills out like music. None of it's for me. I have a mission: make this event planning business thrive, make Charlie Greene a name that echoes in the halls of high society, make it so my curves are synonymous with success and not struggle.

"Charlotte" might be etched on my birth certificate, but "Charlie" is the moniker that carries weight—the persona of a woman who doesn't flinch at challenge, whose ambition is as wide as her hips, and whose practical mind maps out her next move before the current one is complete.

My phone vibrates against the fabric of my pocket again. I sigh as I slip it out, fingers grazing the cracked screen—another expense on the never-ending list. The number is unfamiliar, but in this business, that's the harbinger of opportunity.

"Charlotte Greene," I answer, voice steady, exuding the confidence I meticulously craft.

"Ms. Greene, this is Claudia, assistant to Alexander Bennett."

The name hits like a shot of espresso straight to the veins. Alex Bennett.

The Alex Bennet.

Billionaire CEO, with eyes that command and a reputation that precedes him like a shadow on a sunny day. His world is one I've always viewed from the outside, pressed against the glass like a child at a candy store.

"Claudia," I respond with a practiced calm, even as my pulse begins to race. "What can I do for Mr. Bennett?"

"Mr. Bennett requires your expertise for an upcoming gala. He insists on nothing short of spectacular."

"Of course," I reply, pulse quickening. "I specialize in spectacular." I want to squeal like a high school girl. *Yes, yes, yes!*

"Excellent. Mr. Bennett will expect no less.

Details will follow. Prepare to exceed expectations, Ms. Greene."

"Always do," I say, but the line is already dead, buzzing with the silence of anticipation. I stand rooted to the sidewalk, the world blurring around me. This is it—the break I so desperately need.

Not only could this booking get me close to paying off my start-up business loans, but it could open up doors to better venues.

Higher-paying clients.

Success and stability.

I can't stop the grin that breaks across my face.

I'm going to plan the hell out of this gala.

Chapter 2

Alex

I stand at the edge of the murmuring crowd, a flute of champagne teetering forgotten between my fingers. Sharp jabs about my perpetually single status assault me from all sides. Well-meaning, but they sting all the same.

I'm weary of this conversation—the same one

that's been gnawing at me for years. It's as though my success is nothing without a partner to flaunt.

"Alex, you've got everything—a woman's touch is all that's missing in your life," my sister prods with a nudge that's less playful and more pointed.

"Maybe he's just too picky," chimes in my brother, before he laughs like he's cracked the funniest joke of the evening.

Their barbs cling to my skin. I resist the urge to rub away their expectations along with the irritation that comes with them.

Why is my love life—or lack thereof—anyone's business but my own?

It's not that I don't want a woman. I just haven't found that *one* yet.

Granted, I don't know how I'll know that I've found *the one*, only that somehow I will.

I'll just *know*.

I think.

Fuck, I don't know.

I scowl.

My sister makes another serious remark wrapped up in a teasing tone, but before I can conjure up a retort, my attention snags on something—or rather, *someone*—far more captivating.

There's a goddess standing amidst the opulence of the gala, a striking contrast to the sea of tailored suits and designer gowns. I watch in awe as she holds her hand up to an earpiece, her lips moving urgently.

Those lips…holy fuck. They're wet and glistening with red gloss.

Like ripe cherries…

My cock twitches in my pants as my eyes rove over her heart-shaped face.

Green eyes, dark hair that flows down her curvy back. My fingers twitch at the dip in her back, her waist.

She's all curves and confidence, her dress hugging every inch of her like it was painted on just for her.

Her every move radiates efficiency, the way she glides across the floor with purpose, orchestrating the night's events with an invisible hand.

She must be the event planner I hired. Fucking hell, had I know this sweet thing would be orgaizing everything, I might have taken a more active role in the planning of this evening.

My eyes trace the length of her legs, the swell of her breasts beneath the fabric, a primal appreciation coursing through my veins.

A surge of something darker curls within me, possessive and immediate.

I *want* her.

The intensity of this sudden desire takes me by surprise, the ferocity unlike anything I've felt before. And it's not just her body that has me entranced—it's *everything* about her.

She has this confidence but also this innocence about her.

I tear my eyes off her long enough to pull up my emails. I quickly locate the one with the details about tonight and find what I'm looking for.

Charlotte Greene. Goes by Charlie.

Charlie.

Even her name feels like a puzzle piece clicking into place—a perfect match for the enigmatic woman who now holds my rapt attention.

My heart pounds a rhythm that syncs with the steps she takes, each one echoing the growing need taking root deep within me.

"Excuse me," I say, abandoning my glass on a passing tray with a clatter. The chatter of my siblings fades behind me as I navigate the crowd, intent on one thing.

Get to *her*.

Every instinct tells me what I'm about to do is reckless, but caution has no place here—not when every fiber of my being demands that I know her.

I close the distance between us, my stride confident. She's a vision against the backdrop of opulence—her curves wrapped in professionalism, yet screaming to be unwrapped, and I'm like a kid at Christmas.

"Busy night, huh?" My voice is silk over steel as I lean casually against the marble pillar beside her.

Charlie doesn't miss a beat, her eyes flicking to mine for just a fraction of a second before returning to her clipboard.

"You're handling everything beautifully. It's rare to see someone so...dedicated."

It's as if she finally realizes who I am because her eyes flick back up to mine and she apologizes, "I'm so sorry, Mr. Bennet. I was engrossed in triple-checking the menu."

"Alex," I correct her smoothly, letting my name hang between us like an invitation. "And triple-checking?" I chuckle softly. "Sounds like you're as much of a perfectionist as I am."

Her lips twitch, almost smiling, but she maintains her professionalism. "It's important to me that everything goes perfectly at these events."

I nod, appreciating her diligence and the slight flush on her

cheeks as she speaks. Her commitment is admirable, and it only fuels my curiosity about her.

"Can I do something for you?" she asks, all business.

"Something like that." I flash a grin, but it fades as she remains unmoved, unimpressed. "Have dinner with me."

The words slip out, more command than request.

She blinks and looks startled, but then she quickly recovers, her veneer of professionalism falling back over her face. "Mr. Bennett—Alex—thank you, but I don't mix business with pleasure. It's unprofessional."

My heart falls, and something coils tight in my chest. Panic—an unfamiliar and loathsome sensation—grips me.

I can't let her walk away. The thought alone is intolerable.

"I'll pay you," I blurt out.

Her eyebrows shoot up, and I wince. "Dammit, that came out wrong," I quickly ammend.

"I think I should go—" she turns to walk away, and I damn near have a heart attack.

"Wait," I say, and there's an edge of desperation in my voice I barely recognize."Hear me out."

She pauses, eyebrows raised, waiting.

And I don't know what the fuck comes over me, but I say the craziest, stupidest thing I can think of in a last-ditch bid to keep her from walking away.

I just need to buy more time with her, and I don't give a fuck how I go about doing that.

"Be my fake girlfriend." If possible, her eyes, framed by those thick, beautiful lashes, get even wider. "It's not what you think," I go on. I'm babbling now, and it's pathetic, but fuck, it's the effect this woman apparently has on me. "It's...strategic. For appearances. My family—they won't stop giving me shit about not having a girlfriend."

"Fake girlfriend?" Her voice is incredulous, skeptical. "Why would I—"

"Because I'll pay you a lot," I interrupt, urgency bleeding into my words. "Enough to make any financial worries disappear."

Charlie's expression is unreadable for a moment that stretches too long. Then, slowly, she lowers her clipboard. "How much are we talking?"

"Name your price," I say without hesitation.

"Playing someone's girlfriend isn't exactly in my job description," she says, but there's a new note in her voice.

Thank fuck, she's considering it.

"Consider it a side gig. One that pays exceptionally well." Hope surges through my veins. "What do you say?"

She studies me, her gaze intense and probing. I hold my breath, waiting, needing her to say yes.

Not for the sake of quieting my family, but because the desire to have her by my side—even under false pretenses—has become a craving I can't ignore.

"Fine," she finally says, and relief crashes into me like a wave. "But we set clear terms. This is strictly business."

"Strictly business," I echo, a victorious smile curling my lips.

"Starting now," she adds firmly, extending her hand.

I take it, and a jolt of electricity shoots up my arm from the contact. My cock shoots a spurt of precum from my tip. I feel it stain the inside of my pants.

Christ Almighty, what this curvy beauty does to me.

No way in hell this is strictly business.

Because Charlie is *the one*.

I know it.

www.ingramcontent.com/pod-product-compliance
Lightning Source LLC
Chambersburg PA
CBHW031758150726
47989CB00006B/2786